For I & M
~ J H

À Lou, Paula et Johan mes super futurs voisins,
et Flora qui j'espère les rejoindra
~ L L

LITTLE TIGER PRESS LTD,
an imprint of the Little Tiger Group
1 Coda Studios, 189 Munster Road, London SW6 6AW
www.littletiger.co.uk

First published in Great Britain 2019
This edition published 2020

Text copyright © Jess Hitchman 2019
Illustrations copyright © Lili La Baleine 2019
Jess Hitchman and Lili La Baleine have asserted their rights
to be identified as the author and illustrator of this work
under the Copyright, Designs and Patents Act, 1988

A CIP catalogue record for this book is available from the British Library

Printed in China • LTP/2700/3074/0120

2 4 6 8 10 9 7 5 3 1

In
Every House,
on Every Street

Jess Hitchman

Lili La Baleine

LITTLE TIGER

LONDON

Our house is made out of four walls and a door,
some wonky old bricks and a wobbly old floor.

But I've got a secret. Come this way with me!
I'll show you some things that you can't always see.

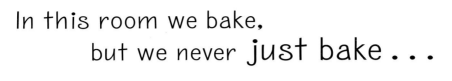

In this room we bake,
    but we never **just bake**...

We sing into spoons and get covered in cake!

We dance in our aprons and taste what we make,
We work as a team when we're learning to bake.

In this room we eat,
        but we never **just** eat . . .

We party like **pirates** and hunt for a treat!
We climb under tables and tickle some feet.
We share lots of giggles
each time that we eat.

In this room we chat,
　　　　but we never **just chat . . .**

We dress up like rock stars and sing to the cat!
We play silly games but it's more than just that,
We say how we're feeling at home when we chat.

In this room we rest,
but we never **just rest** . . .
We slouch on the couch in a big comfy nest!
We talk through our day and get things off our chest,
We figure stuff out while we're getting some rest.

In this room we clean,
but we never just clean . . .

We pull funny faces and try to look mean!
We paint works of art that will never be seen.
We work through our worries
as well as get clean.

In this room we sleep,
but we never just sleep . . .

We hide under pillows and try not to peep!
We build giant castles and count fluffy sheep.
We comfort each other at night before sleep.

In this house we play,
but we never **just play** . . .

We clear up the mess at the end of the day.
We learn to say sorry and wipe tears away.
We love every minute, at home, when we play.

Our street has got chimneys and wonky old bricks,
With windows and wobbly old floors we could fix.
But under the ceilings, behind all the doors . . .

. . . I wonder if our house is rather like yours?

More heartwarming stories from Little Tiger . . .

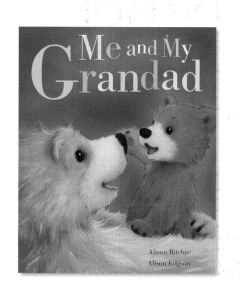

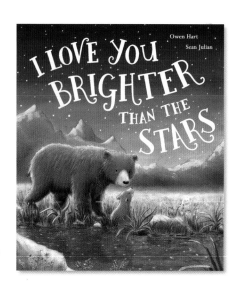

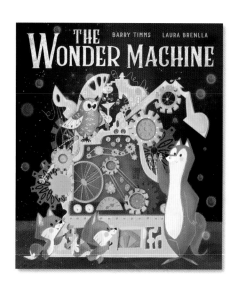

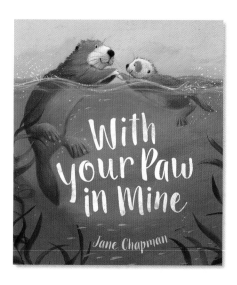

For information regarding any of the above titles or for our catalogue, please contact us: Little Tiger Press Ltd, 1 Coda Studios, 189 Munster Road, London SW6 6AW • Tel: 020 7385 6333 E-mail: contact@littletiger.co.uk • www.littletiger.co.uk